T5-CVE-287

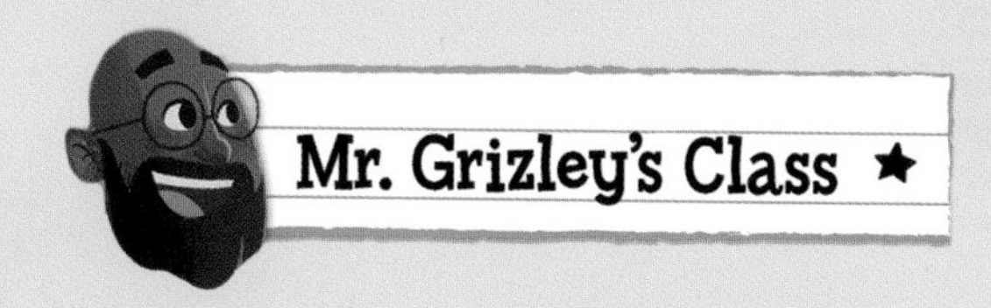

by Bryan Patrick Avery illustrated by Arief Putra

PICTURE WINDOW BOOKS
a capstone imprint

Published by Picture Window Books, an imprint of Capstone.
1710 Roe Crest Drive, North Mankato, Minnesota 56003
capstonepub.com



Library of Congress Cataloging-in-Publication Data
Names: Avery, Bryan Patrick, author. | Putra, Arief, illustrator.
Title: Mordecai's magic / by Bryan Patrick Avery ; illustrated by Arief Putra.
Description: North Mankato, Minnesota : Picture Window Books, an imprint of Capstone, [2022] | Series: Mr. Grizley's class | Audience: Ages 5–7. | Audience: Grades K-1. | Summary: It is Mordecai's first day in Mr. Grizley's class, and before he can really introduce himself it is time for the school assembly--but when the scheduled magic show is canceled Mordecai steps in and reveals that he has brought some magic tricks of his own.
Identifiers: LCCN 2021006181 (print) | LCCN 2021006182 (ebook) | ISBN 9781663910264 (hardcover) | ISBN 9781663920973 (paperback) | ISBN 9781663910233 (pdf) | ISBN 9781663910257 (kindle edition)
Subjects: LCSH: Magic shows—Juvenile fiction. | Magic tricks—Juvenile fiction. | First day of school—Juvenile fiction. | CYAC: Ability—Fiction. | Magicians—Fiction. | Magic tricks—Fiction. | First day of school—Fiction. | Schools—Fiction.
Classification: LCC PZ7.1.A9736 Mo 2021 (print) | LCC PZ7.1.A9736 (ebook) | DDC 813.6 [E]—dc23
LC record available at https://lccn.loc.gov/2021006181
LC ebook record available at https://lccn.loc.gov/2021006182

Designed by Kay Fraser and Dina Her

Printed in the United States 4759

# TABLE OF CONTENTS

Mr. Grizley's Class ★

Cecilia Gomez

Shaw Quinn

Emily Kim

Mordecai Foster

Nathan Wu

Ashok Aparnam

Ryan Clayborn

Rahma Abdi

Nicole Washington

Alijah Wilson

Suddha Agarwal

Chad Werner

Semira Madani

Pierre Boucher

Zoe Charmichael

Dmitry Orloff

Camila Jennings

Madison Tanaka

Annie Barberra

Bobby Lewis

## CHAPTER 1

# First Day

Mordecai set his backpack down on his assigned desk.

"You must be the new kid," a student said. "My name is Shaw."

Mordecai smiled.

"I'm Mordecai," he said.

"Wow!" Zoe said. "Your backpack looks really heavy."

Mordecai patted the backpack.

"I brought a few things I might need," he said. "Just in case."

Mr. Grizley stood up from his desk.

"Class, we have a busy morning," he said. "But first, let's welcome our new student, Mordecai."

“Hello, Mordecai!” the class cheered.

Mordecai waved.

"I'd let you tell us more about yourself," Mr. Grizley said. "But we need to get to a special assembly. As you leave the room, take a look at these."

Mr. Grizley pointed to posters hanging on the walls around the room.

“I’d like you to make one of these, Mordecai,” Mr. Grizley said. “They’re called talent posters. Every student makes one. You draw yourself in the middle and then write or draw your talents around the edges.”

“What if I only have one talent?” Mordecai asked.

Mr. Grizley smiled.

“Sometimes that one talent makes all the difference,” he said.

## CHAPTER 2

# The Bad News

"Okay, class, let's get going," Mr. Grizley said. "We don't want to be late."

"Where are we going?" Mordecai asked.

"A magic show!" Shaw said.

Mordecai grinned. "Great!" he said. "I love magic."

"You can sit with us," Shaw told Mordecai.

Mordecai followed Shaw, Bobby, and Zoe out of the classroom.

The class filed down the long hallway to the auditorium.

Principal Bueno stood at the end of the hall. She did not look happy.

"Bad news," Principal Bueno said. "The magician had to cancel."

The class groaned.

"No magic show?" Cecilia asked.

"Sorry, kids," Mr. Grizley said. "Let's all head back to class."

Mordecai raised his hand. "Mr. Grizley," he said. "I might be able to help."

Mordecai whispered in Mr. Grizley's ear. Mr. Grizley smiled and nodded.

Mordecai ran back to the classroom.

CHAPTER 3

# The One Talent

Mordecai returned to the auditorium carrying his backpack and wearing a bright red cape.

As the students sat back down, Mordecai took his place on the stage.

Mordecai took a deep breath and looked at Mr. Grizley. Mr. Grizley nodded.

“Good morning,” Mordecai said. “My name is Mordecai, and I’m a magician.”

Everyone gasped.

Mordecai opened his backpack. He pulled out a magic wand.

"Abracadabra!" he said.

He waved the wand, and it turned into a bouquet of flowers.

"Whoa! Did you see that?" Emily asked.

Next, Mordecai pulled out a white handkerchief.

"Watch closely," he said. "Abracadabra!"

Mordecai blew on the handkerchief, and it turned into a dove!

"Amazing!" Zoe said.

Mordecai used every trick in his backpack.

For his finale, he pulled out an old top hat. "Abracadabra!"

He flipped the hat, and a bowling ball fell out!

Mordecai took a bow. The students gave him a standing ovation.

"You saved the day," said Mr. Grizley.

"You were right," Mordecai said.

"About what?" Mr. Grizley asked.

Mordecai grinned. "One talent can make all the difference."

BE
KIND

# LET'S MAKE A TALENT POSTER

**WHAT YOU NEED:**

- 1 large piece of paper or poster board
- markers or crayons

**WHAT YOU DO:**

1. Draw and color a picture of yourself in the center of the poster.
2. Write your name at the top of the poster. It can be as creative or fancy as you'd like.
3. Now, write or draw pictures of some of your favorite talents. Have fun! If you're into music, you can draw musical instruments or music notes. If you like computers or video games, you can draw that. You can draw as much as you would like. Remember what Mr. Grizley said: "One talent makes all the difference."

Once you're finished, hang your talent poster somewhere you'll be able to see it. You can take a peek at your poster whenever you need a reminder of your talents and how special you are.

MORDECAI
MY TALENT:
MAGIC

# GLOSSARY

**assembly** (uh-SEM-blee)—a meeting of students and teachers for special learning or entertainment

**auditorium** (aw-dih-TAWR-ee-uhm)—a large room used for gatherings

**bouquet** (boh-KAY)—a bunch of flowers

**difference** (DIF-er-uhns)—an important effect on a situation

**finale** (fih-NAL-ee)—the close or end of something

**ovation** (oh-VAY-shuhn)—enthusiastic clapping and shouting

**talent** (TAL-uhnt)—a natural ability or skill

**whisper** (WIS-per)—to talk very quietly or softly

## TALK ABOUT IT

1. How do you think Mordecai felt before his first day at a new school? Do you think his feelings changed once he met his new classmates?
2. Why was Mordecai nervous about creating a talent poster? If you made a talent poster, what would you put on it?
3. How did Mordecai's classmates feel when the magic show was canceled? Have you ever had to deal with disappointment? What did you do?

## WRITE ABOUT IT

1. Explain how Mordecai's one talent made a difference to the other students.
2. Pretend you are Mordecai and make a talent poster that shows your talent.
3. If you were in Mr. Grizley's class, what talents would you share with your classmates? Make a list.

## ABOUT THE AUTHOR

**Bryan Patrick Avery** discovered his love of reading and writing at an early age when he received his first Bobbsey Twins mystery. He writes picture books, chapter books, middle grade, and graphic novels. He is the author of the picture book *The Freeman Field Photograph*, as well as "The Magic Day Mystery" in *Super Puzzletastic Mysteries*. Bryan lives in northern California with his family.

## ABOUT THE ILLUSTRATOR

**Arief Putra** loves working and drawing in his home studio at the corner of Yogyakarta city in Indonesia. He enjoys coffee, cooking, space documentaries, and solving the Rubik's Cube. Living in a small house in a rural area with his wife and two sons, Arief has a big dream to spread positivity around the world through his art.